The Story of Giraffe

CONCEIVED AND ILLUSTRATED BY
Guido Pigni

WORDS BY
Ronald Hermsen

FRONT STREET Asheville, North Carolina

"**G**iraffe, you must find another giraffe before the flood comes—a girl giraffe, with a long neck and spots like yours. We need a pair. That's how it must be."

Giraffe begins to look for a girl just like him.

"Mouse, Mouse! Have you seen a giraffe lately?"

"A giraffe?" asks Mouse. "You mean with a long neck and spots?"

"Yes, that's it!" says Giraffe.

"I see one now," Mouse says.

Giraffe looks down at his spots and shakes his head sadly.

On the savanna Giraffe sees Elephant.

"Have you seen any giraffes?" he yells.

But Elephant doesn't answer. He just sprays water so far it almost splashes Giraffe.

Giraffe begins to worry about the flood.

"Fish! Will you teach me to swim?"

"Sure," says Fish. "Come on in."

"Can you teach me on land?" asks Giraffe. He is afraid of the water.

Fish moves his fins and tail, and swims from left to right.

"That's all there is to it!" says Fish.

Giraffe feels relieved. He just learned how to swim.

Ostrich has a long neck but no spots. Giraffe digs a hole quickly and sticks his head in.

"Hello! Have you seen any giraffes?"

"It's too dark in here. I can't see anything," Ostrich says.

Giraffe pulls his head out of the ground and walks away slowly, shaking the sand from his mouth, nose, and eyes.

Giraffe walks for a long time until he meets Kangaroo.

"I can't find a girl giraffe, with a long neck and spots just like mine," he says sadly.

"Shall I shorten your neck?" asks Kangaroo.

"Please don't."

"How about coloring your spots, then?"

"That's a better idea," says Giraffe.

The rain begins to pour, and Kangaroo's paints wash away. Giraffe looks the same as always, with a long neck and spots, when he meets Camel.

"Do you know where I can find a girl that looks exactly like me?" Giraffe asks.

"I think you should go that way," Camel says. "Yes, why don't you go that way?"

Giraffe walks and walks. It's very cold!
He has arrived at the end of the world.

No girl giraffes here.

Giraffe loses hope. Will Noah ever let him on the boat without a girl giraffe? He rests his head against the branch of a tree.

"How lonely I am!" he thinks.

Giraffe dreams of all the animals he has met on his journey and of all the animals he did not meet. He cries in his sleep. Nowhere in his dreams is there an animal that looks like him.

Giraffe wakes up suddenly. It is raining harder.

"I must get to the boat," he thinks. "All my friends will be on it. At home I never felt as lonely as I do now."

And he runs ...

But he arrives too late. The boat has sailed.

"I must catch it somehow!" he thinks.

He finds a small boat and jumps in.

The small boat tosses in the wind and the waves,
and fills with water until it begins to sink.

"Help!" Giraffe shouts. "Help!"

But no one hears him.

Giraffe remembers Fish's swimming lesson.
He moves his legs and tail back and forth.
Legs, tail, legs, tail ... it works! Thunder
and lightning split the sky. Giraffe gets very
tired. Up and down, up and down he goes.
Up and down ...

... until a woolly arm slips gently around his neck.

The other animals watch as Giraffe comes aboard.

When Giraffe opens his eyes, he sees animals everywhere: big, small, black, white, colorful, flying, crawling, walking, with short legs, with long legs, with short necks, with long necks, with spots, without spots. Long neck ... spots ... Long neck with spots! A girl giraffe!

"We hoped you'd come back," Noah explains.

Giraffe puts his head against the girl giraffe's cheek. And slowly the boat sails away to blue skies.

For our children, Beatrice, Alessandro, Zoë, Maan, and Niamh,

and for all the children all over the world

The original edition was published by Ankh-Hermes Publishers, Deventer, the Netherlands,
under the title *Het verhaal van Giraffe.*
Copyright © 2006 by Uitgeverij Ankh-Hermes bv Deventer

Library of Congress Cataloging-in-Publication Data
Pigni, Guido.
[Verhaal van Giraffe. English]
The story of giraffe / conceived and illustrated by Guido Pigni ;
words by Ronald Hermsen.
p. cm.
Summary: After learning that he cannot board Noah's ark
until he finds a girl giraffe to go with him, Giraffe asks other creatures
for help but, while they teach him valuable lessons, none can
help with the main problem.
ISBN-13: 978-1-932425-87-1 (hardcover : alk. paper)
[1. Giraffe—Fiction. 2. Noah's ark—Fiction. 3. Animals—Fiction.]
I. Hermsen, Ronald. II. Title.
PZ7.P6252Sto 2007
[E]—dc22
2006012531

FRONT STREET
An Imprint of Boyds Mills Press, Inc.
A Highlights Company
815 Church Street
Honesdale, Pennsylvania 18431